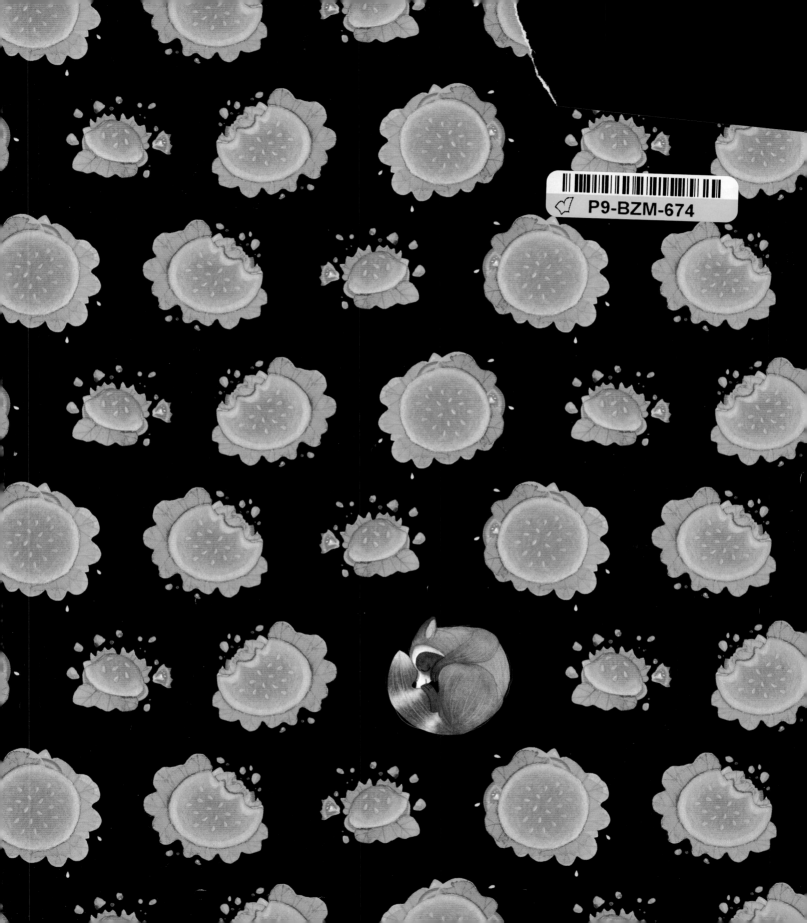

FOR BEATRICE:
better than all the cheeseburgers,
more special than all the sunrises

Katherine Tegen Books is an imprint of
HarperCollins Publishers.

Are You a Cheeseburger?
Copyright © 2021 by Monica Arnaldo

ISBN 978-0-06-300394-1

The artist used watercolor, colored pencils, and ink
to create the digital illustrations for this book.
Typography by Amy Ryan
21 22 23 24 25   SCP   10 9 8 7 6 5 4 3 2 1
❖

First Edition

MONICA ARNALDO

ARE YOU A
CHEESEBURGER?

KATHERINE TEGEN BOOKS
An Imprint of HarperCollins Publishers

This is Grub.
Grub is a raccoon,
and he is all by
himself.

See?

And here is Seed. Seed is a seed, of course, and he is stuck in the trash.

This particular seed and this particular raccoon had very little in common.

Except, at that moment, they were both in the same garbage can.

"Hello," said Seed.

Grub continued rooting around.

"Oh, you are busy. That is all right.
I am busy too."

Grub stopped. "You are?"

"I am looking for someone to plant me
in the ground so I can start growing."

Grub eyed the seed hungrily.
"Will you grow *food*?"

"I am not sure," Seed admitted.

"Could you grow cheeseburgers?"

"What is a cheeseburger?"

Grub considered this. "Something very good and very special."

"Hmm . . . maybe. We will have to wait and see."

Grub had never seen a
cheeseburger plant before. . . .

But he liked the sound of it,
so he planted Seed right away.

The two spent every evening together, from moonrise to moonset. Grub tried to be patient. But Seed began to wonder: What if he wasn't a cheeseburger plant? What if he was something else entirely?

To help pass the time, they told stories. Grub told Seed about the top three cheeseburgers he had ever eaten.

1. Half a cheeseburger, barely moldy.

2. A piece of cheeseburger bun with some mustard on it (wrestled away from seagulls).

3. A greasy paper wrapper Grub could tell had once contained a cheeseburger.

Seed told Grub about all the interesting things he saw down in the earth.

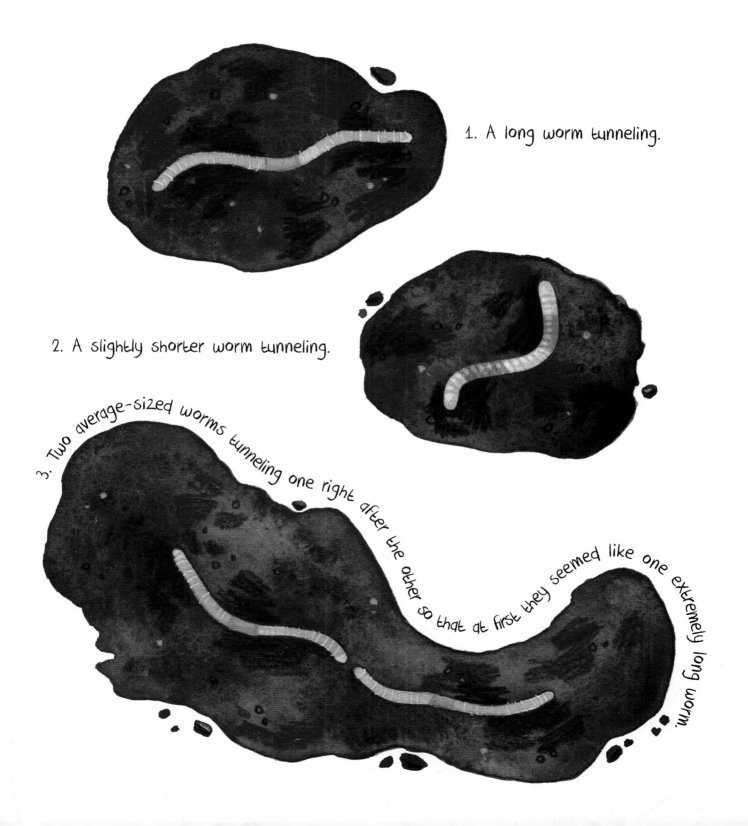

1. A long worm tunneling.

2. A slightly shorter worm tunneling.

3. Two average-sized worms tunneling one right after the other so that at first they seemed like one extremely long worm.

"What is happening down there?"
Grub asked.

Seed looked around. "It is dark.
What is happening up there?"

"It is dark, too. Later, though, the sun
will rise."

"What is that like?" Seed asked.

"I am not sure," Grub confessed.
"I am always asleep then. But I have
heard that it is like a cheeseburger:
very good and very special."

Both alone in the dark, Grub and Seed tried
to picture the sunrise.

Slowly,

s l o w l y,
things began to change.

"Hello again," said Seed.

"Seed! You are out of the ground!"

"Yes," said Seed proudly, "I am growing."

That evening, Grub and Seed celebrated.
Grub had a greasy piece of cardboard
he was almost certain had once been the
bottom of a pizza box. Seed had water.

"To the future!"

Sure and steady, Seed kept growing.
And growing.

The cheeseburgers were nearly at hand.

Finally, one morning just before sunrise . . .

. . . Seed bloomed.

"Oh," said Seed.

"Are the cheeseburgers ready?!" asked Grub.

"Grub," Seed started, "I do not think I am a cheeseburger plant. . . . I think I am just a flower."

"A flower?"

"Yes."

"Not a cheeseburger plant?"

"No."

"So . . . no cheeseburgers, then?"

"No cheeseburgers."

Grub was quiet for a long time.

"What is it?" Seed asked.

"I am thinking," Grub said.

"About cheeseburgers?"

"No. About flowers."

"Oh. What are you thinking about flowers?"

"I am thinking that flowers are good and special, too—maybe even more special than cheeseburgers."

"More special than cheeseburgers?" Seed gasped.

"Well. The same."

This is Seed.
Seed is a flower.
See?

And this is Grub.
Grub is a gardener.

They don't have any cheeseburgers,
but they do have each other. And *that*
is something very good and very special.